About this book

Many children have difficulty puzzling out letters because they
are abstract symbols. Letterland's worldwide success is all about its
enduring characters who give these symbols life and stop them from
being abstract. In this book we meet the Quarrelsome Queen. Her story is
carefully designed to emphasise the sounds that the letter 'Q' makes in words.
This definitive, original story book is an instant collector's classic,
making learning fun for a new generation of readers.

A TEMPLAR BOOK

This edition published in the UK in 2008 by Templar Publishing
an imprint of The Templar Company plc,
The Granary, North Street, Dorking, Surrey, RH4 1DN, UK
www.templarco.co.uk

First published by Thomas Nelson & Sons Ltd, 1993
Devised and produced by The Templar Company plc

ISBN 978-1-84011-781-3

Printed in China

Classic LETTERLAND Storybooks

Quarrelsome Queen's Quiz

Written by Stephanie Laslett

Illustrated by
Maggie Downer

templar publishing

It was breakfast time at the Palace, and Quarrelsome Queen was in a very bad mood.

"This toast is burnt!" she grumbled to the King.
"It's nicely browned, dear," said Kicking King, mildly.

"No, it's burnt, I tell you! Completely burnt!" shouted Quarrelsome Queen.
"Let's not quarrel over a silly thing like toast," said the King quietly.

"I wasn't quarrelling," said the Queen.
"Yes, you were," said the King.
"No, I wasn't!" the Queen shrieked, banging the table with her fist.

Luckily, a fanfare of trumpets stopped the Queen's quarrel. In marched a messenger with a letter on a velvet cushion.

"Royal Mail delivery for Quarrelsome Queen," he announced grandly, handing the Queen an envelope.

"It's a letter from my sister," said the Queen, tearing open the envelope. "She is sending her children to stay with us this weekend."

"What! Polly, Poppy, Peter and Paul?" asked Kicking King. "That's FOUR children. What a quantity!"

"**W**ell, of course there are four of them," replied Quarrelsome Queen crossly. "They are quadruplets, all born on the same day."

"No wonder she wants some peace and quiet," murmured Kicking King.

The next day Quarrelsome Queen went to collect the quads from the Letterland Station. The train was just pulling into the platform as the royal car arrived.

Quarrelsome Queen had no trouble spotting them. They all looked exactly the same – apart from Peter who had freckles.

"**Q**uick, into the car with you all," she ordered. "And if you're good you'll find a nice cake waiting for you at the Palace."

"How big is it?" asked Poppy.
"What kind is it?" asked Peter.
"When can we eat it?" asked Paul.
"Where can we eat it?" asked Polly.

"Too many questions!" said the Queen. "It's very large, it's chocolate, and you can eat it in the kitchen as soon as we get home."

The quads squeaked with delight.
They squeezed quickly into the back of the car.

When they arrived at the Palace, a large, square chocolate cake was waiting for them on the kitchen table.

As soon as they saw it, the quads all started squealing excitedly.

"Can we eat it outside?"
"Can we eat it inside?"
"Where are the plates?"
"Where is the knife" they all asked at once.

"Be QUIET!" shouted Quarrelsome Queen. "Otherwise you will not get any cake."

That made the quads quieten down.

"Good!" said the Queen. "Now you can cut the cake into quarters. One piece for each of you."

For a moment everything was quiet as each quad carefully cut one quarter. Then the shouting began again.

"Your quarter is bigger than my quarter!" complained Polly.
"No it isn't. Your quarter is bigger than mine," replied Poppy.
"My quarter is too small!" wailed Peter.
"I want a different quarter!" squawked Paul.

Quarrelsome Queen covered her ears with her hands.

"**Q**uiet, QUIET please," shouted the Queen. At that moment Kicking King strode into the kitchen.

"Stop! Stop!" he cried. "There has been too much quarrelling today."

For once the Quarrelsome Queen agreed with the King.
"What we need is some peace and quiet," said Quarrelsome Queen firmly. "Do you quarrel all the time?" she asked the quads.

"No, we ask questions, too," replied Polly. That gave the Queen a splendid idea.

"**I** know the best way to keep you quiet," said the Queen. "You can answer some questions for a change. We will have a Quiet Quiz!"

"What a good idea," whispered the King to himself. "Quite brilliant!"

"Follow me!" cried the Queen. The quads formed a queue behind her as they all went upstairs into the Queen's Quiet Room.

"Now, this quiz is going to be all about my friends in Letterland," explained the Queen. "Let's see how many answers you know."

"Who has a hundred hats?" asked the Queen.

Paul scratched his head. Was it Clever Cat?

Polly thought hard. Was it Sammy Snake?

Peter gazed at the ceiling. Was it the Yo-Yo Man?

Poppy put up her hand. "I know, I know!" she cried. "The Hairy Hat Man has a hundred hats!"

"Quite right," said Quarrelsome Queen. Poppy looked very pleased.

"Now for my next question. Who fights fires in Letterland?"

Polly frowned. Was it Lamp Lady Lucy?

Poppy scratched her nose. Was it Bouncy Ben?

Paul stared at the floor. Was it Robber Red?

Peter put up his hand. "Me! Ask me!" he cried. "Fireman Fred fights the fires in Letterland!"

"Quite right," said Quarrelsome Queen.

"Now for my last question. Who likes to quarrel – but found out today that peace and quiet is much better?"

"We know! We know!" shouted all four quads together. "It's you, Quarrelsome Queen, it's you!"

"Quite right," laughed Quarrelsome Queen. "Now I think I prefer quizzes to quarrelling, don't you?"

And do you know, the quads thought that she was quite right!

THE END